Come Home Already!

By Jory John

Illustrated by Benji Davies

HARPER
An Imprint of HarperCollinsPublishers

Yeh!

I know an old lady who swallowed a dog
My, what a hog to swallow a dog
She swallowed the dog to catch the cat
Swallowed the cat to catch the bird
Swallowed the bird to catch the spider
That wriggled and jiggled and tickled inside her
She swallowed the spider to catch the fly
But I don't know why she swallowed the fly
I guess she'll die

I know an old lady who swallowed a goat
She just opened her throat and swallowed the goat
She swallowed the goat to catch the dog
Swallowed the dog to catch the cat
Swallowed the cat to catch the bird
Swallowed the bird to catch the spider
That wriggled and wriggled and tickled inside her
She swallowed the spider to catch the fly
But I don't know why she swallowed the fly
I guess she'll die

I know an old lady who swallowed a cow
I don't know how she could swallow a cow
She swallowed the cow to catch the goat
Swallowed the goat to catch the dog
Swallowed the dog to catch the cat
Swallowed the cat to catch the bird
Swallowed the bird to catch the spider
That wriggled and wriggled and tickled inside her
She swallowed the spider to catch the fly
But I don't know why she swallowed the fly
I guess she'll die

I know an old lady who swallowed a horse
She's dead, of course

Animal Alphabet Song

A's for the Ant, and
B's for the Bee
C's for the Cat, and
D for Doggie

E's for the Elephant
F for the Frog
G's for the Goose, and
H for the Hog

I-J-K come next in line
But these we'll skip
For they're difficult to rhyme

L is for the Lamb, and
M is for the Mule
N's for the Nanny-goat
O for Owl

P is for Polecat
Q for the Quail
R for the Rat, and
S for the Snail

U and V come next in line
Skip these two just to save a little time
W is next and stands for Whale
X is a Cross, and
Y has a tail
Z is for Zebra
It can't be wrong
And that is the end of this silly little song

C
D
E
G

Heel, Toe, and Away We Go

Franky went away to France
He went to learn the polka dance
First, we start with heel and toe
And then three hops and away we go
Heel, toe, and away we go
And heel, toe, and away we go

Wendy went to Washington
To visit friends and have some fun
There she met the President
He shook her hand and away he went

Heel, toe, and away we go
And heel, toe, and away we go

Tommy went to Timbuktu
To see the animals in the zoo
How he laughed to see a bear
A-rocking in a rocking chair

Lucy went to London Town
To see the King put on his crown
Then she met the King's ladee
Who asked her in for a cup of tea

Harry went to Hudson Bay
Away up north in Canaday
There he saw a great big whale
And he went riding on its tail

Randy Boone went to Rangoon
To find and catch a big baboon
All he found were lots of ants
They got into his shirt and pants

Mary went to Montreal
To attend a fancy ball
There she met a nice young man
But he was shy, and away he ran

Hally went to Hollywood
To star in movies, if she could
But she never got a chance
She couldn't sing and she couldn't dance

Debbie went to Delaware
She met a handsome fellow there
He said: "Will you marry me?"
And she accepted happily

Caleb went to Calgary
The big rodeo for to see
Rode upon a cowboy's horse
And had a lot of fun, of course

Sally sailed across the sea
Until she came to Italy
There she went to visit Rome
And see the Pope upon his throne

Freddy went to Florida
The sunniest place he ever saw
On the beach the people lay
And watched him swim and play all d

Maxine went to Mexico
To see a grand fiesta show
It was such a great delight
To sing and dance all day all night

Now you've heard this song of mine
Why don't you try to make a rhyme
Don't be shy to take a chance
And don't forget the polka dance

123 ABCD

One, two, three, four, five, six, seven
Stars are twinkling up in heaven
Eight, nine, ten, eleven, twelve
You can sing it now yourself
One, two, three, four, five, six, seven
Stars are twinkling up in heaven

A B C D E F G
H I J K L M N O P
Q R S T U V
W X Y Z
Now you've heard my ABC
You can sing along with me

A B C D E F G
H I J K L M N O P
Q R S T U V
W X Y Z
Now you've sung my ABC
It's as easy as can be

My Father's in the City

My father's in the city, the city, the city
But he'll be home today
He's bringing me a fiddle
And this is how I'll play
Zing, zing, zing, zing, up on the little fiddle
Oh, this is how I'll play

My father's in the city, the city, the city
But he'll be home today
He's bringing me a trumpet
And this is how I'll play
Tataratatara, up on the shining trumpet
Oh, this is how I'll play

My father's in the city, the city, the city
But he'll be home today
He's bringing me a trombone
And this is how I'll play
Waah-waah, waah-waah, up on the sliding trombone
Oh, this is how I'll play

My father's in the city, the city, the city
But he'll be home today
He's bringing me a clarinet
And this is how I'll play
Doodle, doodle, doodlet, up on the gentle clarinet
Oh, this is how I'll play

My father's in the city, the city, the city
But he'll be home today
He's bringing me a tuba
And this is how I'll play
Pwaah-pwaah, pwaah-pwaah, up on a great big tuba
Oh, this is how I'll play

My father's in the city, the city, the city
But he'll be home today
He's bringing me a flute
And this is how I'll play
Up on the silver flute

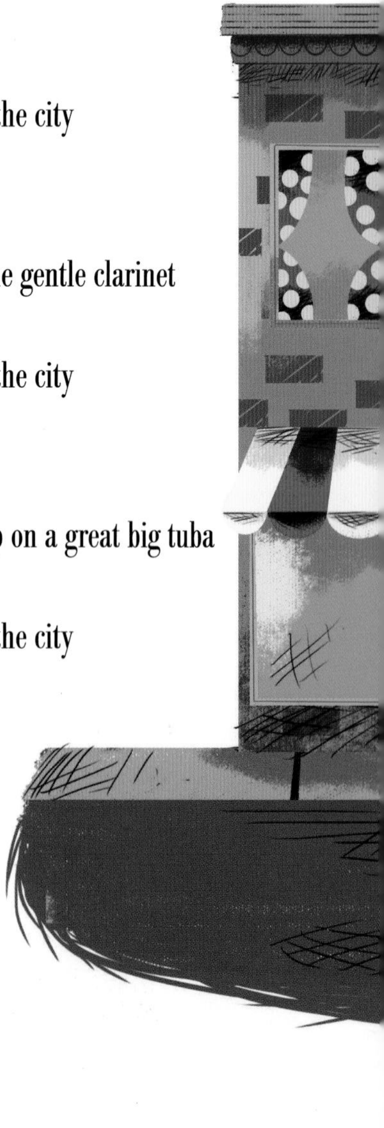

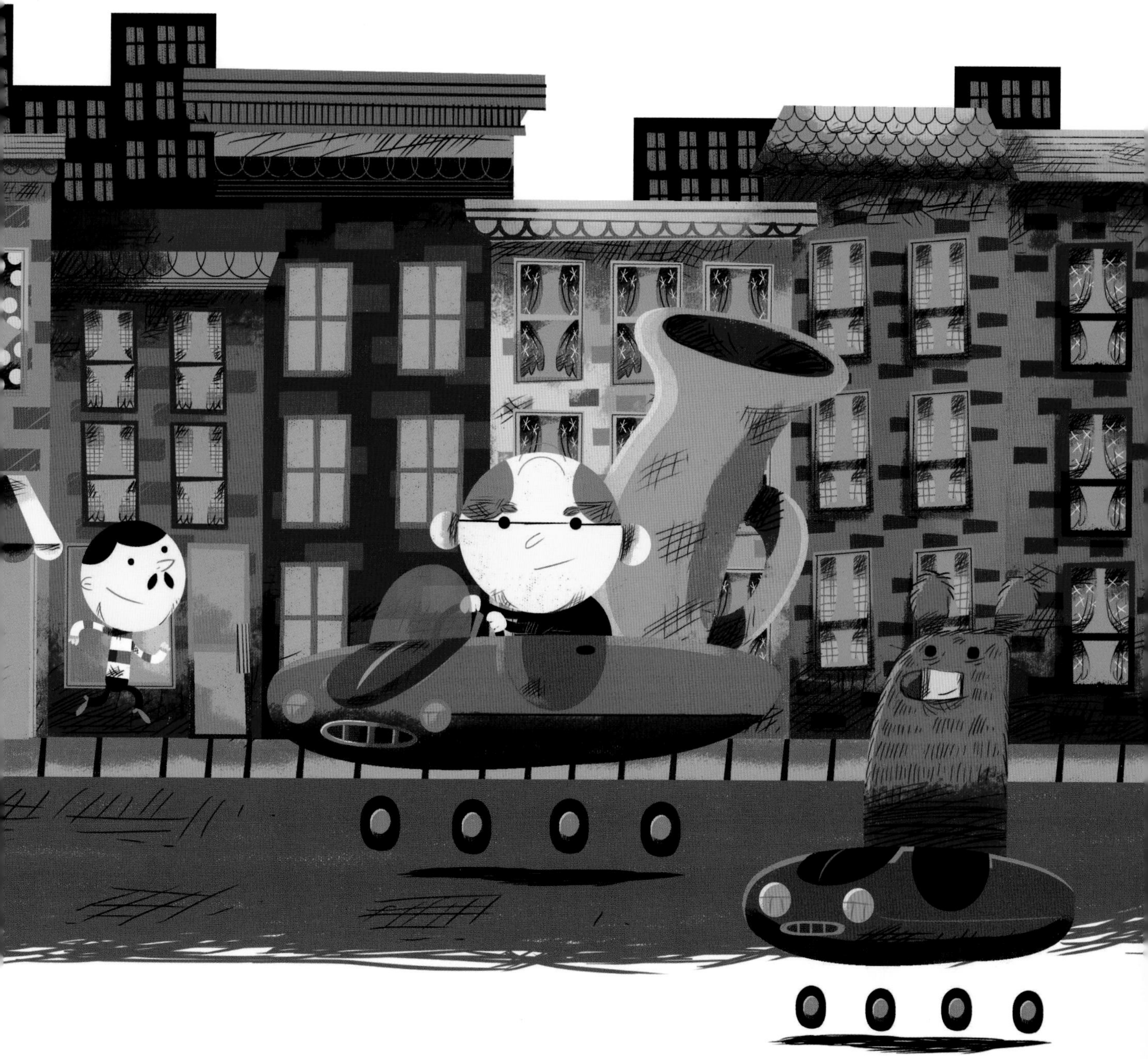

Sailing Over the Sea

To Boston Harbor came a ship
Sailing over the sea
After a long and weary trip
Sailing over the sea
Sailing over, sailing under
Oh, the crew came down by number
With a one, two, three
Sailing over the sea

The first was sailor number one
Sailing over the sea
Chewing upon a crusty bun

The next to come were sailors two
Sailing over the sea
Riding upon a kangaroo

The next to come were sailors three
Sailing over the sea
Each of them with a sack of tea

The next to come were sailors four
Sailing over the sea
All of them danced upon the shore

The next to come were sailors five
Sailing over the sea
Into the harbor they did dive

The next to come were sailors six
Sailing over the sea
Three with shovels and three with picks

The next to come were sailors seven
Sailing over the sea
All of them bearded and unshaven

The next to come were sailors eight
Sailing over the sea
Carrying monkeys in a crate

The next to come were sailors nine
Sailing over the sea
Each of them with a cask of wine

The next to come were sailors ten
Sailing over the sea
They never went to sea again!

Once I Had an Old Red Hen

Once I had an old red hen
And what said the old red hen?
"Cluck-cluck-cluck," said the old red hen
Till she laid an egg
And then, started clucking once again

Once I had a rooster grey
And what said the rooster grey?
"Cockadoodle-doo," at the break of day

Once I had an ugly duck
And what said the ugly duck?
"Quack, quack, quack, I have no luck"

Once I had a lovely goose
And what said the lovely goose?
"Quonk, quonk, quonk, go turn me loose me loose"

Once I had a yellow cat
And what said the yellow cat?
"Meow, meow, meow, there is a rat"

Once I had a dog, so black
And what said the dog, so black?
"Ruff, ruff, ruff, don't scratch my back"

Once I had a lazy sheep
And what said the lazy sheep?
"Baaa, baaa, baaa, I want to sleep"

Once I had a Jersey cow
And what said the Jersey cow?
"Moo, moo, moo, come milk me now"

ZZZ..

Per Fiddler

There once was a farmer
Who had a fine cow
He wanted to fiddle
But didn't know how
He had no violin

One day he decided
To trade his fine cow
He traded her in
For a fiddle and bow
A fine, old violin

His neighbors all said
It was really a sin
To trade a fine cow
For a an old violin
An old, old violin

But then, when he started
To fiddle away
His neighbors soon saw
That he knew how to play
That old, old violin

The called him "Per Fiddler"
And started to dance
And soon the whole village
Was caught in a trance
Of that old violin

Per Fiddler, he played
And the violin sang
Made everyone dance
Till the cobblestones rang
That dear, old violin

Then each of the neighbors
He wanted to trade
And offered him wealth
For the fiddle he played
That dear, old violin

Oh no, said Per Fiddler
That would be a sin
You keep all your wealth
I'll play my violin
My dear, old violin

The Hungry Goat

There was a man
Now please take note
There was a man
Who had a goat
He loved that goat
Indeed he did
He loved that goat
Just like a kid

That goat was born
So I've heard said
With two small horns
Upon his head
He had a beard
Upon his chin
And the whitest coat
You've ever seen

When he was young
He was so small
You'd hardly think
He ate at all
But he ate so much
It was a fright
No one could touch
His appetite

All day he chewed
And chewed and chewed
For all he saw
He thought was food
He nibbled grass
And leaves and twigs
And even stole
The swill from pigs

He swallowed flies
And bugs and bees
And chewed the bark
Of many trees
And other things
Like paper bags
And bits of strings
And dirty old rags

And chicken feathers
And flour sacks
And old shoe leather
Complete with tacks
And rubber tires
From used up cars
And broken glass
From bottles and jars

Though you may think
That I'm a liar
I swear he loved
To eat barbed wire
And rusty nails
And old tin cans
And pots and pans
And frying pans

Now that there goat
He grew and grew
Until he reached
Just five-feet-two
But still he grew
And grew some more
Until he got
To six-feet-four

His master rode
Him everywhere
To rodeos
And county fairs
He always won
The biggest prize
For there was none
To match his size

His master was
So proud of him
He was so proud
It was a sin
Then trouble came
And he got mad
And what he did
Was very sad

That hungry goat
One morning fine
Ate three red shirts
From off the line
His master grabbed
Him by the back
And tied him to
A railroad track

Now when a train
Came into sight
That goat became
Pale-green with fright
He heaved a sigh
As if in pain
Coughed up those shirts
And flagged the train

Now when the train
Came to a stop
The engineer
Called for a cop
They took that goat
To the country jail
And there they held
Him without bail

While waiting there
To hear his fine
That hungry goat
Began to pine
For all he got
To eat each day
Was a bit of straw
Or dried-up hay

His hunger grew
Till, with a moan
He began to chew
That wall of stone
He chewed and chewed
Clean through the wall
And thus escaped
And fooled them all

The goat, he ran
Without a stop
Until he came
To a bakery shop
And there he saw
Before his eyes
A pile of dough
Set out to rise

Now of that dough
He had a feast
How could he know
It was full of yeast
And when the dough
Began to rise
That goat blew up
To twice his size

He looked just like
A big balloon
As he floated off
Bound for the moon
Now, of this tale
This is the end
For no one saw
That goat again

Sing a Little Song Along With Me

Sing a little song along with me
It's a pretty simple melody
Anyone can sing it easily
Sing a little song along with me

Everybody sing
Let your voices ring
Now we've got it right
So, sing with all your might

Twelve Kittens

Oh, once I had twelve kittens
One day, one went up to heaven
And that left me only eleven

Once I had eleven kittens
One was frightened by a hen
And that left me only ten

Oh, once I had ten kittens
Then one day one drank some wine
And that left me only nine

Oh, once I had nine kittens
One slipped through the garden gate
And that left me only eight

Oh, once I had eight kittens
Then I sent one off to Devon
And that left me only seven

Oh, once I had seven kittens
One ate too much candy sticks
And that left me only six

Oh, once I had six kittens
In the lake one took a dive
And that left me only five

Oh, once I had five kittens
One ran off to the butcher store
And that left me only four

Oh, once I had four kittens
One day, one sailed off to sea
And that left me only three

Oh, once I had three kittens
One got lost in my old shoe
And that left me only two

Oh, once I had two kittens
One was stricken by the sun
And that left me only one

Oh, once I had one kitten
Off to London she did run
That's the end, my song is done

6
5
Butcher
4
7
3
8
Devon
2
1

The Months of the Year

January is the month when every year begins
Sometimes it is very cold with bitter freezing winds
February's much the same, as everybody knows
Unless you live in places where it never ever snows

Then comes March with warming breezes melting ice and snow
April follows with its rains to help the flowers grow
May is such a merry month, for all the earth's in bloom
Then comes the most romantic month, the lovely month of June

In July, it's hot and dry, in August it's the same
Then we have September with it's soft and cooling rain
Colder is October, when the leaves begin to fall
While farmers work at harvesting their crops to feed us all

Windy is November, when our summer trees go bare
That's when we remember to give thanks in song and prayer
Lastly comes December, with its merry Christmas cheer
As we prepare to enter into one more brand new year